Secrets of Songbird Cottage (Pleasant Bay Book 4)

Sylvia Price

Penn and Ink Writing, LLC

Stay Up to Date with Sylvia Price

Subscribe to Sylvia's newsletter at newsletter.sylviaprice.com to get to know Sylvia and her family. It's also a great way to stay in the loop about new releases, freebies, promos, and more.

As a thank-you, you will receive a FREE exclusive short story that isn't available for purchase.

Praise for Sylvia Price's Books

"Wow, what a great start to a new series, and I really enjoyed reading it as it was so well-written, and I can't wait to read the next book. This is the first book that I have read by Sylvia Price but not the last and I recommend you read it and you will not be disappointed."

"Author Sylvia Price wrote a storyline that enthralled me. The characters are unique in their own way, which made it more interesting. I highly recommend reading this book. I'll be reading more of Author Sylvia Price's books."

"I love the way this is a very real example of one of the beauties of these small towns! Of course, mixing in beautiful scenery and the growing love with an old friend makes this the perfect start to a new series!"

"I've read several books written by Sylvia Price; she has done a great job at writing a good short story; she is becoming one of my favorite authors. I can't wait to read more of books her books."

"The storyline caught my attention from the very beginning and kept me interested throughout the entire book. I loved the chemistry between the characters."

"The plot flows easily, and the characters are appealing. It's a great story that shows what is most important in life."

"A wonderful, sweet and clean story with strong characters. Now I just need to know what happens next!"

"I just could not put this book down. Thank you for a delightful read."

"I love Sylvia's books because they are filled with love and faith."

"Sylvia's books ooze with love and goodness."

Other Books by Sylvia Price

Jonah's Redemption: Book 1 – FREE

Jonah's Redemption: Book 2 – Available on Amazon

Jonah's Redemption: Book 3 – Available on Amazon

Jonah's Redemption: Book 4 – Available on Amazon

Jonah's Redemption: Book 5 – Available on Amazon

Jonah's Redemption: Boxed Set – Available on Amazon

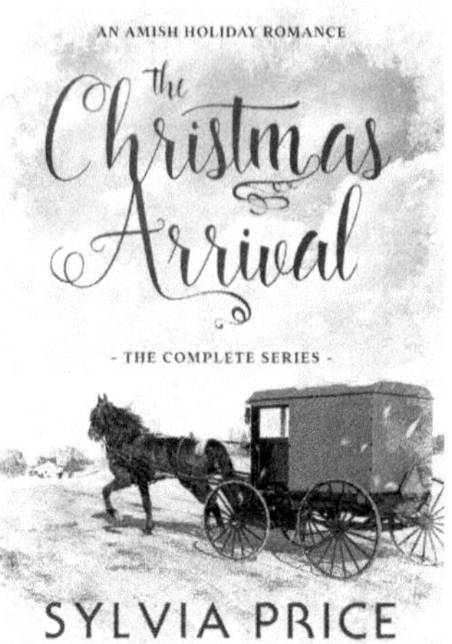

The Christmas Arrival – Available on Amazon

Contents

Chapter One: So Cozy in Your Arms

Claire Havisham was happy to experience her first winter at Cape Breton. The tiny island's latitude might be considered more northerly than Nova Scotia itself, but it still enjoyed a temperate coastal climate that neither rose too hot in summer, nor dipped too cold in winter—just like Goldilocks' porridge!

As she sat comfortably before a blazing log fire at Songbird Cottage, Claire thought back to all the balmy summer vacations she had spent there as a child with her mother, Emma, and her little sister, Izzy. In those days, it had been an exciting adventure to drive along Cabot Trail Road, seacoast on one side and dark forests on the other, such a change from the gray metropolitan landscape of Manhattan. When the rental car would pull up on the crackling gravel driveway that led up to the cottage's front door, the girls would bound out of the car and run to see if the flowers they had planted the previous summer had bloomed. A swath of nodding purple coneflowers and marguerite daisies would greet them, butterflies and large bees fluttering and humming with activity.

Then suddenly, they had stopped visiting Pleasant Bay every summer. Claire had been fourteen years old and had wanted to stay close to her friends during the vacations. Going anywhere with her parents had become "lame" and "boring." Her school breaks couldn't be anywhere that wasn't, at most, a few blocks away from a shopping mall or trendy clothing store. Holidays and school semesters were grudgingly spent either at her father's luxurious mansion in Halifax or with Emma at her Tribeca apartment.

Why didn't my thoughts turn more often to our old vacation home? Why did I let superficial teenage pursuits get in the way of visiting the island?

The thought of Songbird Cottage lying alone and neglected off its quiet, weaving country lane, made Claire feel sad. For nearly eighteen years, the little converted barn had stood waiting for someone to find shelter under its vaulted roof. Its surrounding flower beds had blossomed and withered with no one to notice or appreciate them. Her father, John, and his second wife, Linette, had been too absorbed in their own lives to pop over to Pleasant Bay. They had made the move from Manhattan to Halifax; in part, because Linette wanted to be as far away from Emma as possible, but mainly because John wanted his elderly parents to be close by so he could look after them.

Occasionally, John would remember to call a gardening and home maintenance service in Halifax and pay them a substantial amount to cross over the Canso Causeway and make the five hour drive up the northwestern top of Cape Breton, to tidy things up in and around the cottage. For the rest of the year, Izzy and her bunch of crazy Manhattan musician friends, would have free rein over the place whenever they went up there to party.

Claire picked up her phone to check the latest messages. She always left the notification alert off as there was just something about Songbird Cottage that was incompatible with electronic noise, but she wanted to see if Richard was on his way.

Richard Benson was a lawyer in Sydney, shared primary care-taker of his mother who had Alzheimer's, and the love of Claire's life. They had been together since Claire had left Bangor and moved into Songbird Cottage. Every weekend and Wednesday, Richard would drive across to Pleasant Bay to spend time with Claire. They were both firm believers in quality, over quantity, time. When Claire would hear the sound of Richard's tires squashing the gravel, as his car drove up outside, her stomach would skip and lurch with a bubble of excitement.

Should be there at about eight-thirty. Just helping my dad bathe Mom and put her to bed. Love you. See you soon. R xxx

After reading the text message, Claire jumped up to check on the chicken pieces she had taken out of the freezer that morning. Some of them were still partially frozen. She placed the plated chicken on top of the stove and turned on the oven.

What is it about chicken that lends itself so easily to being half thawed and half frozen? I wish Dad hadn't warned me about food poisoning all the time. It makes me paranoid!

John Havisham was a doctor. His professional concerns had always bled over into his family life.

Claire pricked up her ears and went to the window to peek out. She had heard the sound of a car arriving. It was too early to be Richard. The moon was already glowing in the evening sky and illuminated Emma's hatchback pulling up as close to the front door as possible. Its small tires had left narrow grooves in the snow. Claire saw Emma bundle up her fake, fur-lined hood when the car's interior light came on and open the driver's side door.

Emma was always popping by to visit her eldest daughter. She had once called Songbird Cottage home, but now she lived with her husband, Sam, at the brewery down the road. Emma's winters were usually spent helping Sam with his beer, coffee, and honey mail order business. She also loved creating beautiful websites for the crafts people and artisans on the island. If things got busy, she would sometimes ask Claire to come and help out.

"Oof!" grunted Emma, as she pushed the front door open, "your father should *really* build a mud room here instead of having all this patio space. Where are we expected to leave our boots?"

Emma bent down to brush a few flakes of snow off her boots, and then proceeded to unlace them. "Can I just dump them here?" She pushed the boots into a corner next to the kitchenette work surface. "At least no one can fall over them then."

Claire smiled as she responded, "Mom, you had no complaints about this *summer* holiday cottage when you lived here!"

Emma gave her daughter a grudging smile in return. "Point made. But with all your father's millions, you'd think he would make this place habitable for winter."

"That's not fair, Mom. You told Dad you used some of your auction money to have the exterior double glazed when you lived here. See, it's warm as toast inside," Claire protested.

"Triple glazed, actually," Emma corrected as she moved to switch on the kettle, "so the cottage is ready for this February freeze."

"Dad says the cold fronts pass quickly, and most of the snow comes in January," Claire replied, "so maybe that's the reason he hasn't added an entrance hall. Spring is only one month away, y'know."

Emma poured herself a mug of instant cocoa and sat down next to Claire on the low-seated velvet sofa. "I came to find out if any more anonymous gifts have arrived for you."

Claire shook her head, "Nothing since the last one, Mom. They were arriving like clockwork during the fall, and then I got a big one for Christmas. That was the antique jewelry box I showed you. A courier showed up with a box of candy in January. But so far, nothing for February."

"It's still early in February," Emma said, "and did you remember to ask the courier about the sender's address, like I told you to do?"

Claire sighed, "It's just some random business postal address, similar to the ones scam mail order companies use. The gifts are definitely not from anyone in the Bondi family or Giulio—it's not his style." Claire alluded to her ex-boyfriend and his extensive family in Bangor, back in Maine.

Emma looked concerned. "I still think you should tell Richard about them. I know for a fact that Kate uses a private investigator for some of her cases. Maybe he could dig something up for us." Kate was Richard's partner at their law firm and very possibly John's girlfriend, but Claire's father was keeping their relationship under wraps until his divorce from Linette was finalized.

"I want to keep Richard, Kate, Dad, and anyone else, out of this, Mom," Claire stipulated adamantly. "You might think it's threatening for me to receive anonymous presents, but I don't. What's the harm?"

Emma couldn't quite put her finger on why she'd had a feeling of foreboding when her daughter had told her about the strange parcels, flowers, and messages that had begun to arrive at Songbird Cottage last year. Claire had been eager to leave Bangor behind and relocate to Songbird Cottage after her beauty salon had been trashed. There was nothing left for her in Maine anymore.

All of her friends chose to side with Giulio after their breakup, which made sense as they had all originated from him in the first place.

Claire had packed up a few things she'd needed from her apartment and driven back to Cape Breton with Richard. She hadn't looked back, figuratively or literally, since then. Within one week of setting up home at the cottage, the first courier had arrived carrying a huge bouquet with a card.

"Now that you are finally free, you know it's time to be with me."

The writing on the card wasn't familiar. Claire had called up the florist from where the bouquet had originated.

"People call in or order online, and our flower arranger is the one who transcribes the message onto the card, ma'am. I'm sorry I can't tell you more. Credit card details are private."

The helpful assistant had sounded genuinely sorry. Claire had thanked her and pressed disconnect. The mysterious bouquets and gifts had continued arriving at irregular intervals over the next five months. The messages that accompanied them were all the same.

Claire was very close to her mother and they had no secrets between them, but when Claire had told Emma about the deliveries, her mother had freaked out. Emma's anxiety levels had been on edge since then. It just didn't seem right to her that some stranger was sending what amounted to love letters to her daughter.

"Who are they? How do they know where you live? Giulio and his overbearing mother have agreed to move on since you declined to press charges after his mom drove her car through your salon's window. So, who is doing this?"

"Who, who, who. You sound like an owl, Mom," Claire declared in exasperation at her mother's nagging, "It's probably an old boyfriend from college. People can find out anything they want off social media nowadays, y'know."

Emma looked at her beautiful daughter and remembered how complete she'd felt the day she had held that tiny baby girl in her arms. She remembered how Claire's blaze of red hair had made the nurses in the maternity ward coo with admiration. She shivered when she thought of some person lurking in the shadows, sending their unwanted presents.

The crunch of gravel outside let the two women know that Richard had arrived.

"No! I forgot to put the chicken in the oven!" Claire yelled as she ran over to the oven, popped the tray of chicken in, and cranked the dial up high. "Hush about those stupid gifts now, please, Mom. I don't want Richard thinking I come with drama. Goodness knows he's had to endure enough nonsense from sorting out the Bondi trouble for me."

Claire ran to the sunken bathroom at the back of the cottage and checked her makeup. It was not a moment too soon. The sound of Richard's spare key in the lock could be heard, and he soon walked into the cottage. His face lit up when he saw Claire emerging from the bathroom. She ran to Richard with a beaming smile on her face and wrapped her arms around him, tightly.

"It's so cozy in your arms, love," she murmured.

After returning her embrace with gentle tenderness, Richard turned to greet Emma.

"Hey there, Emma. It's nice to see you. How's Sam and brewery life treating you?"

"All good, thanks for asking." Emma was very fond of Richard, and already considered him to be family.

Richard shook his head when Claire offered to make him some tea. "No thanks, darling." He hesitated before continuing, "I'm glad your mom is here, actually, because I have something to tell you—and I don't want anyone getting upset."

Emma and Claire froze and waited to hear what Richard was about to say.

"My fiancée arrived in Sydney today," Richard announced.

Chapter Two: Is It On, or Is It Off?

"**R**ichard…" Claire squeaked, "what on earth do you mean, 'fiancée'? Your dad would've mentioned this to me when I've been to visit. Are you joking?" Emma had her arms folded and she, too, wore a severely judgmental expression.

Richard held up his hands and moved to go and sit at the dining table in the middle of the room. "I'll explain everything," he said.

"You better," Claire spluttered as she sat down opposite him. "Come join us, Mom. I'm sure you won't sleep tonight until you know what's going on."

Richard waited until everyone was settled and then began his explanation.

"I met Geneviève while I was studying at McGill. I was lonely as a result of focusing solely on my studies through to my final year. That made me ripe for falling in love with the first pretty face that came along. It just happened to be Gen. She's lived in Montreal all her life, and being with her gave me access to a life outside of my cramped living quarters. Also, the drudgery of working part-time stopped me from hanging out with the other students."

Richard leaned across the table and took hold of Claire's hand. "I know you'll understand it when I say that falling into the *habit* of being with someone is a very easy thing to do—and it's completely different from falling in *love* with someone. That's what happened with Gen. She became a habit."

"How long did it go on for?" Claire hated herself for asking the question, but she couldn't stop herself doing so.

"That's where things get complicated," he confessed.

Richard went on to explain to Claire and Emma how he had been swept up into Geneviève's world. Spending weekends with her family—in between studying and working at his part-time job—he'd found it both comforting and indulgent to arrive at the sprawling Le Plateau-Mont Royal home and be warmly welcomed by Gen's mother, Madame Allaire. The Allaires were strict Catholics, so he'd been allowed to stay in the pool house at the bottom of the garden whenever he'd visited. Nighttime was spent holding hands with Gen in the entertainment room, watching movies on the widescreen television and eating homecooked meals. To a lonely young man with his closest family off from the mainland, it had been heaven.

"It was only after I finished law school and passed the bar that things became more complex," Richard continued, "because it was generally presumed that Gen and I would get married. Her father pulled some strings to get me into a prestigious law firm in Montreal, and when those salary checks started coming in, it made me even more complacent about things!"

It had been the perfect arrangement for a young, ambitious lawyer. Richard could work long hours and live in relative sparse accommodation, as the Allaire home was always open to him.

Over the passing years, the money had begun to pile up in his bank account after his student loans were repaid, and it had seemed reasonable to buy Gen an engagement ring with some of it. The fact that she never pushed for a live-in arrangement suited Richard just fine. They would occasionally meet at his tiny studio apartment for an awkward liaison, but then she would have to return to the house at Le Plateau-Mont Royal before her parents became suspicious. It had worked well enough, until Mère and Père Allaire had confronted Richard.

"They wanted me to set a date for the wedding. They said Gen was in her late twenties and needed to settle down with a husband and children of her own. All of her brothers and sisters were already married, so…" Richard played with the salt and pepper shakers on the table, pushing them around each other.

"What did you do?" In spite of herself, Claire was interested in Richard's story. It reminded her about the fact that countless young people all over the world were manipulated into getting married every day. She would know how to recognize those sorts of situations because it had nearly happened to her as well.

Richard sighed and pushed his chair back from the table slightly.

"By that stage, my mom was already well into her early onset dementia, and I will say this much for my dad; he knew how hard things would become and how rapidly the dementia could progress, but he never hesitated in his decision to care for her."

Claire patted his hand lovingly. Richard's father, Bo Benson, was his mother's other primary caretaker. He was holding the fort at the Bensons' sweet little nautically-themed home in Sydney, so that Richard could visit Songbird Cottage.

Richard looked down at the table, saying, "I wanted to look

after my mom, and I also wanted to get out of my obligation to marry Gen. By that stage, I knew we had no fireworks together. That spark of intense desire and love had just never ignited." He looked at Claire when he said this, and she knew he was referring to the almost instant attraction they had felt for one another when they had first met last fall.

"It's always better to leave someone if you think you don't love and care for them anymore. It's either a case of absence making the heart grow fonder, or out of sight, out of mind!" Emma interjected.

"I agree," Richard said. "I began looking for job opportunities in Sydney and found Kate's notice. I was upfront with her, saying I couldn't bring a letter of recommendation with me because the law firm where I worked was affiliated with Papa Allaire.

"I took the bull by the horns once I had Kate's letter of appointment and went to Chez Allaire to break the news to them. I sugar-coated it as much as I could. Said I wanted to go and look after my mom and believed I would have too much on my plate for marriage. I told Gen she could keep the ring and left."

There was silence in Songbird Cottage after Richard finished explaining. The smell of roasting chicken filled the room, and Claire felt her tummy rumble.

"Why has she come here, then?" Claire probed as she rose from her chair and went to check on the oven. The chicken looked crispy and golden. Maybe a few minutes more and it would be done.

"I thought I'd been as clear as I could be, but I guess I wasn't." Richard, too, rose from the table and went to the hutch to remove plates and cutlery from the drawers, adding, "She says we're still engaged, and that if I don't come back to Montreal, then she wants to move to Sydney to help me look after my mom."

"How delusional—and altruistic—of her," Claire said, her voice heavy with sarcasm.

"No one could be *that* delusional," Emma huffed, "you must have done or said something to encourage her, Richard."

Richard's eyes widened at Emma's accusation. "I swear, I never encouraged her, Emma! She arrived at my parents' house, and I rushed back home as soon as my dad texted me to say she was there. He says she waggled her ring finger under his nose when he opened the door, and said, pleased to meet you—I'm Richard's fiancée.' What was he meant to do?"

"She sounds a bit crazy," Claire commented as she brought the tray of chicken and a pasta salad to the table and took a seat.

"I'm not buying it," Emma said emphatically, "you're going to have to do better than that, Richard. Is your relationship with this woman on or off?"

Richard swallowed his mouthful, before replying, "Here's my phone, Emma. You can open all my messaging apps, emails, anything you like. The only communication I've had with Gen lately was to wish her and her family a joyeux Noël et bonne année."

Emma took Richard's proffered phone and scrolled through it while Claire and Richard ate their dinner.

After several tense minutes, Emma pushed the phone back toward Richard and nodded her head. "Sorry I was skeptical, Richard. I had a bad experience with my second husband, and it's made me distrustful. So, what do you plan to do?"

Richard took a sip of his tea before saying, "She's staying in my parents' guest room tonight, and I would like Claire to come back with me to Sydney tomorrow, so we, as a couple, can break the news to Gen that I'm not available anymore."

"Ooh-wee, I'm not going to be looking forward to that encounter," Claire asserted. "She must be absolutely besotted with you to burn a candle for this long."

Richard shook his head, "Uh-uh, I don't think it's that. I think it's because she's stubborn and spoiled. I think she'd been expecting me to return to her for the last year, all humble and penitent. And when I didn't, her pride couldn't take it, so she's taken matters into her own hands."

Emma shrugged her shoulders as she pushed herself back from the table. "Rather you than me, guys. It's getting late, and Sam will be wondering what's happened to me." She gave Claire a hug from behind before moving to the wall where her boots lay. "Give me a call or text when you arrive in Sydney, Bear. I want to hear all the grisly details."

Emma walked out of the door with a wave of her hand and shut it quickly behind her.

"Mom's taking this more seriously than she lets on," Claire told Richard, after she'd turned back to him after staring for a while at the closed front door, "because she always calls me 'Bear' when she's concerned about me."

Richard got up to help Claire clear away the remnants of their meal. "I can't blame her, darling. It sounds bogus, even to my own ears."

Claire gave a shrug. "I'm sure this can be handled in such a way that everyone walks away with their dignity intact. Do you think that's possible?"

Richard shot Claire his most charmingly optimistic smile and encouraged, "With you by my side, darling, what could possibly go wrong?"

Chapter Three: Not a Good Combination

"I have to clean the house a bit before we leave, love," Claire informed Richard the next morning. "I don't know how long this thing with Gen might take, and I don't want to come back to mold climbing out of the bread bin to welcome me home."

Richard grabbed a bottle of eco-friendly scourer from underneath the kitchen sink, saying, "I'll help you do it, and don't worry—we don't have to make an early start as I'm sure my old man can handle things until we get back there."

Claire was left alone with her thoughts as she cranked up the vacuum cleaner and the noise made it impossible for any conversation.

I know Richard loves me; I have no doubts on that score. But I can't stop thinking about what he said about his relationship with this Gen woman; that she was equivalent to a bad habit. Is it likely that the same thing could happen to us?

Claire was glad that Richard was in the sunken bathroom under the main bedroom mezzanine level, and he wasn't able to see her deep frown.

It's best for us to get to Sydney, so I can see things for myself, before I start worrying about whatever is being cooked up by my imagination.

Songbird Cottage was looking as spruce as a five-star bed and breakfast by the time Richard and Claire were ready to leave. Claire took more time than usual packing her clothes, makeup, and shoes in a bag. She realized that a flannel shirt or two, jeans, mascara, and winter hiking boots were definitely not going to instill confidence in her before she encountered Richard's old flame. She hemmed and hawed a bit, and then folded in some leggings and a sexy mohair pullover that draped provocatively off one shoulder. A pale tan pair of sheepskin-lined indoor-wear boots and her favorite perfume completed her mobile wardrobe.

I'll take my entire makeup bag and give myself a pedicure in the car while we drive there. I've been so happy with Richard that I've let my grooming slide a bit. All I do when I'm expecting him to arrive is shave and shower. Well, that's about to change!

Claire swept her glorious red hair behind her back and said to Richard in a resolute tone, "En avant, mon amour!"

Once she had locked the door to Songbird Cottage, Claire noticed the solitude brought on by the snow and how quiet the countryside became when blanketed in snow. It seemed to her that the little cottage stood solitarily among the bare trees and bushes, with no one and nothing else for miles around. She breathed in the crisp, cold air and it exhilarated her. Claire heard the car's mechanism go 'ke-lup' as Richard deactivated the locks. With one final panoramic look around at the snowflakes and snowdrifts winking bravely underneath the sun's pale rays, Claire hopped into the passenger side door that Richard was holding open for her.

"Thank you," she said gratefully.

Richard still treats me like a princess. I am so lucky and blessed to have him in my life. Nothing will ever come between us. I'll make double-sure of that.

Richard got in beside her after she'd leaned over to open his door for him from the inside. He smiled his thanks, started the engine, and then backed out of the driveway, his head tilted to see his way behind him in the rearview mirror.

"Whoa," Richard said, "What's this?"

Claire craned her neck to see around the head rest. A large delivery van had pulled up across the driveway exit and stopped. The delivery man had already exited the driver's seat and circled to the back of the van to open up the doors and remove something. She felt a sinking feeling in her stomach. It might be time for some questions and answers, and they hadn't even set out on their journey back to Sydney yet.

"Did you order something online?" Richard asked, before exiting his side of the car; his hand clutched the door handle as he awaited her reply.

Claire delayed answering him to first ascertain exactly what would emerge from inside the van. Maybe she could get around replying to his question truthfully if the delivery man was taking out a plain box. No such luck. The man straightened his back, shut the van doors with one hand, and then made his way up the driveway, clutching a large bouquet of red roses.

"Er, no. I didn't order anything online," Claire prevaricated.

"Then they must have gotten the address wrong," Richard surmised, and got out to walk and meet the delivery man in the driveway.

Claire was too scared to get out of the car. She saw Richard hold his hands out in an attempt to stop the delivery man from coming all the way up the drive for nothing. The man's face was obscured by the huge spray of red rosebuds, but he was able to peer around to speak to Richard, jostle the bunch of flowers into the crook of his left arm, and offer Richard his touchscreen to read the delivery details. Richard bent his head to read the touchscreen. Then he signed the screen casually with his finger and took the flowers the man held out to him. The man accepted the tip Richard offered, touched his hat in a salute, and returned to his van.

Claire saw Richard search among the long-stemmed red roses for a second. He located the accompanying note, scanned it, and tucked it back inside the flowers. Then Richard walked calmly back up the driveway toward the car. His face looked grim.

He opened the backdoor, threw the flowers onto the seat behind him, and then settled himself behind the steering wheel.

"'You and me are meant to be together,'" Richard quoted the bouquet's note. "Not only is it bad grammar, but it's also slightly confusing that you received something so blatantly romantic from someone other than me."

It wasn't a question. It was a statement. A fact. Claire dipped her head and hid her face from Richard with the long sheaves of her hair. Richard pulled the handbrake hard to release it and backed out of the driveway at a significant speed. The delivery van had disappeared into the distance, leaving only its tire tracks in the snow. Their car seemed to be following the grooves it left behind in its wake, pursuing the crushed imprints in the snow like a bloodhound out for blood.

The silence in the car seemed to stretch out for ages, but, in reality, it was only a minute or two before Claire shook back her hair and turned to look at Richard. His handsome profile looked foreboding, and Claire knew she owed him the full truth.

"I don't know who is sending me flowers, Richard. These kinds of deliveries started as soon as I moved to Songbird Cottage. First it was flowers, then candy, then little gifts—one of those mail-order porcelain dolls, a bottle of my favorite fragrance, and a jewelry box—and now it seems to be back to flowers again. Each time the notes inside say kind of the same thing, 'we are meant to be together now that you're single'. But I'm not single, that's what's making it all so confusing."

Richard didn't look mollified at all by Claire's revelation. "And you never thought to bring this up with me before, why, exactly?"

"Mom said I should tell you—ask for your help in trying to find out who is behind it. It's not my ex, Giulio. He's already in college in Colorado, studying anthropology and living a happy student life. I've just shrugged it off, honestly." Claire bristled slightly and became defensive. "And besides, I didn't sign up for telling you every stupid thing that happens to me! Is it so inconceivable that someone would want to send me presents? Am I so ugly that you can't believe the concept of me having a secret admirer?"

Richard kept his eyes steadily on the road after Claire's outburst. He still looked grim, but Claire got the feeling his stern countenance was no longer directed at her.

"I know you would never cheat on me or encourage another man's advances. Heck, you don't like to flirt with the old manager down at that restaurant we go to, even when he offers you a drink on the house, but the person who's sending you these presents knows what your favorite fragrance is—and not even I know that yet!"

Claire gave Richard a shy smile. She had always been prickly when it came to encouraging men or looking for male attention. "I'm a monogamist, through and through, love. You're everything a girl could wish for."

"But you've missed the point here," Richard continued, after acknowledging Claire's compliment with a smile of his own, "you have a stalker. Whoever it is, they have succeeded in disguising this fact from you so far, with cryptic messages and obviously, lovely presents, but you are being stalked. This person knows you've broken up with Giulio, they know you've left Bangor, they have a very good idea about your likes and dislikes, they know where you live now, and they are presuming you live alone—which, for the main part, you do. How on earth can you be complacent about this execrable breach of your privacy?"

Claire felt tears spring to her eyes as she listened to what Richard was saying.

Oh. He's right. How could I have been so blind and foolish?

Noticing her tears, Richard reached over and took hold of Claire's hand.

"Darling, I'm sorry if I sounded accusatory after those flowers arrived. But maybe that delivery arriving when I was there to receive it is a sign that you should be taking this more seriously. And, also, sharing more about what goes on in your life with me?"

Claire replied dolefully, "I didn't want you thinking I came with a whole lot of problems and drama, Richard. After what happened with the Bondis in Bangor, I just wanted us to live in peace. Telling you about those stupid presents would have ruined that."

Richard gave Claire's hand a loving squeeze, and then he put his hand back on the steering wheel, "Never mind about that, darling, I love any drama that you bring. In fact, I don't think that I would be able to recognize you without it."

They both laughed, and Claire felt a surge of love for Richard—and his practical advice.

"Tell me everything about these deliveries, from start to finish," Richard requested, "Perhaps we can work out who this pest is."

Claire felt herself relax. It was rather nice to be able to unburden herself to Richard and seek his opinion on the whole thing. Gen's arrival, and her claim to hold her ex-fiancé to his promise, seemed to fade away as Claire recited back to Richard the same details that she had given her mother.

"So, let's see if I've gotten this straight," Richard summarized after Claire had finished telling her story, "there is no plausible return address, they started coming as soon as you came back here, and the messages indicate a fair amount of knowledge regarding your new circumstances?"

Claire nodded.

"'Now that you are finally free,' —that shows they have been waiting a long time for you to break up with Giulio, so they knew you either before you even started dating him, or during the seven years you were together."

"I never thought of it that way before," Claire said, "but, yes, likely."

"'It's time for you to be with me;' that confirms that you have never been *with* this person, although, in terms of what capacity they are referring to, I can't say. Could be that you did their nails once or gave them a massage? Sometimes, that's all it takes for someone to become obsessed."

Claire thought a while, and then shrugged, "I've seen hundreds of clients in my time as a beautician, and I can spot the weirdos immediately. They book frequent appointments and overstep proximity boundaries all the way. We have a list of warning signs to look for—coming back into the treatment room and finding them completely naked, inappropriate touching or comments. Look, I'm not going to lie, it happens. But I either ban them from the salon or pass them over to one of my freelancers. It's not rocket science."

Richard still looked bothered. "There's just something about those last words I find ominous. It sounds creepily dictatorial and commanding—and that's not a good combination."

Claire clapped her hands together loudly, "Exactly! Now, can we please talk about something else? Before I turn into a complete gibbering wreck and stay locked in my room for the rest of the year."

"I can't tell you about the number of times women have come into the attorneys' offices where I worked, asking for restraining orders or legal protection notifications. There's danger out there, Claire, and you might be looking at it right on the backseat of our car."

"Tchoh!" Claire scoffed, "the only danger I'm in right now is you driving over a bump just when I'm about to paint my toenails this delicious shade of hot pink."

Chapter Four: Geneviève Has an Ace Up Her Sleeve

The car pulled up smoothly outside the Benson residence just over two hours later. Claire pulled the sun visor down and carefully redid her makeup, before considering herself ready to face Geneviève.

"My dad texted me when we were crossing on the ferry, saying he's gotten a cab to take Gen to a nearby hotel," Richard said when he noticed what she was doing, "so there's no need to panic just yet."

"That's actually a relief to hear," Claire said with a smile, "but how do you know I wasn't putting on lipstick to impress your parents?"

When Bo Benson opened the front door, he saw Richard and Claire giggling as they removed their bags from the trunk of the car. Then, to his amazement, Claire pulled an enormous bouquet of red roses out from the backseat and walked to the door with them in her arms.

"Did Valentine's Day come early this year?" he asked the couple as they entered the warm entrance hall gratefully and began kicking off their boots.

"For you, it has," Claire said, giving Bo an affectionate hug, "but if you're worried you missed it, Valentine's Day is still in three days' time."

"I'll take these through to Brigitte," Richard's father said, with a lop-sided grin, "She'll be ecstatic to receive such a beautiful bunch. Can I tell her they come from me?"

"Knock yourself out, Dad," Richard said as he blew warm air onto his hands, "those flowers are from Claire's secret admirer."

"I'm surprised she hasn't got more than one," Bo said, as he followed them through to where Richard's mother was sitting in her usual place, staring out of the bay window in the open plan living room.

Mrs. Benson turned around when she heard people come back into the room. Her vacant expression informed them that his mother was having another memory lapse. Richard and Claire braced themselves to see if she remembered who they were, or not. With every room re-entry or visit, it was necessary to check first and see if Brigitte would be happy to see them or act confused and aggressive, as though they were strangers.

Bo placed the flowers delicately on an end table, and walked forward to sit beside his wife, "Do you remember Claire, 'Gitte? She's our son's girlfriend. She's come to visit."

Brigitte Benson stared hard at Claire, and said, "But she left just now. I saw her get in a cab outside the window. She was staying in the guest room and you said you didn't love her anymore, Richard. What's she doing back here?"

Everyone shifted uncomfortably at Brigitte's words. Richard took a deep breath, and tried to clarify things for his mother, "That was my ex-fiancée, Gen, Mom. Er…she's out here in Cape Breton visiting us, to say hello."

"Who is?" Brigitte gazed at Claire, "This girl or the other one?"

"I think you better go and wash the journey off yourselves," Bo said apologetically, "I'm sure your mother will get the hang of things sooner or later." He moved to reach the bouquet and presented them to his wife with a flourish, "Look what I've brought you, 'Gitte! The most beautiful hothouse flowers!"

Claire and Richard left the room thankfully, but not before they heard Mrs. Benson say, "I heard you say 'there goes trouble,' Bo, when Richard's girlfriend got into the cab you called for her. Why would she come back so quickly if she's trouble?"

Claire went to the bathroom to blow off some steam. She splashed cold water on her cheeks and reveled in its biting temperature on her hands and face. She gazed at her flushed complexion in the mirror sternly.

I wish skeletons would simply stay in their closets sometimes! My stalker rears his ugly head in front of Richard. This jolly Geneviève pops up when and where she's least wanted. Why, oh why can't Richard and I be left alone to be in love, in peace?

Fortunately, Claire realized true life was never uncomplicated, and that could make it equally interesting, or difficult. Richard was right. Her secret admirer could very well turn out to be a very unwelcome irritant. And as for Gen—well, she was next up on the list to be dealt with.

As these thoughts tangled Claire's mind in a confusing web, the doorbell rang loudly in the hall. Claire couldn't help but give a small jump. The words Richard had said to her about danger lurking in hidden corners had sunk in deeper than she knew.

Claire heard Bo whisper to Richard in the entrance hall, "Honestly, I saw her get into the taxicab myself not one hour ago, Son. I have no idea what she's doing back here so fast. This is your problem, and you must confront it and sort it out! Your mother can't handle all of this activity."

Claire opened the guest bathroom door to see Bo pushing Richard forward to open the front door. Richard straightened his shoulders, cleared his throat, and opened the door.

"Gen, come inside, why don't you. It's freezing outside. You'd be much warmer in your hotel room, y'know."

Claire got her first glimpse of Geneviève Allaire as the young woman stepped over the threshold and straightened after untying her bootlaces. There were a few snowflakes stuck in her middle-parted dark brown hair, and the cold weather had given her cheeks a rosy glow. She had a pretty, heart-shaped face, wide-set hazel eyes, and a small, rosebud mouth. She could not have been more than five foot two inches tall, and when her height was combined with her curves, she appeared slightly dumpy and squat.

Maybe it was all the winter clothes she was wearing, but even after removing her overcoat, scarf, and jacket, Geneviève still made Claire think about hobbits and dwarves from the movies she'd watched as a child.

It's probably because I'm tall and willowy that I think she looks so short. It's no wonder Richard spent so often on the sofa watching television with her when they were together, because if they'd been standing up, he'd have gotten tech neck from bending down to look at her all the time.

Claire tried hard to paste a confident smile on her face, and she hoped it didn't appear as false to others as it felt. Geneviève had already pushed passed Richard and Bo in the entrance hall and was making a beeline for the living room. She stopped short when she saw Claire standing at the guest bathroom doorway.

"Is this the new friend you were telling me about, Richard?"

Geneviève had the most delightful accent. Her voice dipped and trilled sweetly, sounding more like the garden birds back at Songbird Cottage, than a grown woman.

Claire stepped forward and held out her hand. "Hey, I'm Claire Havisham, Richard's girlfriend," she casually mentioned to stake her claim.

Geneviève kept her hands snugly inside her sweater pockets. Smiling blandly, she replied in brusque, business-like tones, "I'm afraid that's not possible, you see, Richard is engaged to me."

Gen sounded so emphatic that Claire got the impression there must be a team of lawyers and notaries sitting in the taxicab outside, just waiting to pounce with oaths and briefs to back up her statement.

Bo took charge of the situation when he saw Richard was standing in the entrance hall with a look of dumbfounded concern on his face.

"Come now everyone, let's go and sit in the formal dining area—I don't want this contretemps upsetting 'Gitte. Come along now, chop-chop."

Bo held his arms out on either side, like a territorial swan giving warning signs, and ushered the trio into an elegant dining room opposite the living area. He waited to see them all settle in chairs around the table; Richard at the head of the table, with Claire and Gen flanking him, and then he firmly closed the glass doors behind him and went back to sit with his wife.

There was silence for a few uncomfortable seconds. Then Geneviève opened her mouth to speak. "I apologize for any discomfort you may be experiencing, what is your name again? Claire, is it? But men, eh, they have the most disappointing memories. It seems as though Richard has forgotten he is engaged to *me*, and also, he seems to have forgotten to tell *you* about me, his fiancée." She gave a little shrug of her plump shoulders and continued, "Men, *hein*, they are so naughty."

Richard reached over and took Claire's hand. In that instant, the awkward triangle at the table twisted, with Claire and Richard forming a solid base and Geneviève becoming the sharp point at the top.

Richard, giving Claire's hand a squeeze, said, "If you can remember back that far, Gen, and I'll forgive you if you can't, I told you over one year ago that I didn't want to get married. I allowed you to keep the engagement ring, in accordance with section three, part one of the nineteen-seventy Commission Draft Bill and Act pertaining to breach of contract. You will also recall that you acquiesced to the dissolution of our engagement on the condition you keep the ring, along with certain jointly owned items, to wit: our CD and DVD collection, sporting equipment, and other sundry gifts, all in your possession at the time."

Geneviève's hands lay lightly clasped on the table, but they balled into tight fists at Richard's speech. She glanced down as though calculating her next words carefully, and when she did so, Claire became aware that Geneviève Allaire was possibly shrewder than she let on.

"That is not true. You had to leave for a while to look after your mama. I have been patient long enough, Richard. I have been telling my parents you are returning for me any day now, because deep in my heart I know you still love me. I'm prepared to forgive you for all this,"— here she flicked her hand out toward Claire —"but please stop making me look a fool."

Richard scoffed, "I need to brush up on my legal knowledge about seventy-two-hour lockdowns for the insane."

Claire blanched as Geneviève burst into tears.

Richard rose, moved to Gen's side of the table, and placed his arm around her, patting Geneviève softly between her shoulder blades. It only made her sobs and cries grow ever louder. She grabbed hold of the arm Richard had draped around her for comfort and used it to leverage herself out of the chair. The next thing, Gen was in his arms.

Richard kept patting and comforting Geneviève. This affecting tableau was positioned sideways to Claire's view. She could see Richard turn his head to one side so that the top of Gen's hair wouldn't get in his mouth. When he did this, Claire saw Geneviève's face poke out from between Richard's chest and his upper arm. Even though Gen was wailing and sniffing in a manner fit to raise the roof, Claire saw her eyes and cheeks were absolutely dry. Gen opened her eyes a fraction to see what kind of effect her tantrum was having on Richard, saw Claire watching her, and a coldly calculating look descended over her face. She gave Claire a smirk, and then nestled her face back into Richard's arms.

Claire felt her whole body go cold.

This is far more serious than I first thought. We need to get this woman out of our lives as soon as possible. She's obviously some kind of psycho.

Richard felt around in his pockets, located a tissue, and passed it to Geneviève. She took it gratefully, murmuring, "You are too, too kind," and used it to wipe her fake tears away.

"Wouldn't it be better to go back to the hotel, Gen?" Richard enquired considerately. "You can have a lie down, and maybe you'll feel better afterwards."

Gen gave a doleful sniff, saying, "Please can Claire accompany me back to the hotel? It would bring me much comfort to have another young woman to hear my side of the story. About—about how much I love you."

Richard gave a quizzical glance at Claire across the table.

Claire couldn't think of one thing she would rather do less than to experience a cab ride with this manipulative crackpot, but she nodded at Richard encouragingly.

An Uber driver was summoned on Richard's app while Gen visited the guest bathroom to "pull herself together." This gave the couple time to have a quick whispered conversation.

"What on earth! She's faking, Richard. I saw she wasn't even crying. It was just a lot of hysterical noise."

Richard leaned in close so there was no chance of Gen over-hearing him, "She's been through a lot, Claire. Try to have some empathy, please. Just escort her back to the hotel and make sure she stays there this time. I can't have my mom upset by this racket."

All the grievances and suspicions that were boiling inside Claire's chest disappeared when he said this. Brigitte Benson must come first. Her mental health was precarious enough as it was, without adding a bunch of screaming to it.

The Uber driver gave a honk from outside, and Claire walked out of the dining room to find Gen already tying up her boots and shrugging into her overcoat. Claire hurriedly did the same. Both women turned to say goodbye to Richard before going out the door.

"Au revoir, mon cher," Gen said sweetly.

"See you later," huffed Claire.

The two women went outside, walked down the pathway, and entered into the Uber together. Geneviève pushed in first.

When the two girls were settled and the driver had confirmed the hotel to which they were heading, Gen turned to Claire conspiratorially, saying, "Thank you for accompanying me. Can you keep a secret? I need to have Richard back as my husband because we have a baby together."

Chapter Five: Holding All Four Aces or Not?

I really don't think I can take much more of this day. It started out with Richard and me cleaning the cottage. So how did I end up discussing a baby he might have with his fiancée or ex-fiancée —I really don't know any more—before supper time?

Claire remembered her mother's words of wisdom. It had been the mantra they had grown up hearing: 'thoughts, before words, before deeds.' Claire rubbed her eyes with trembling fingertips as she searched for every reserve of patience and serenity that she could find within herself.

She looked up to see Geneviève carefully observing the effect her words had had on Claire. It was that crafty look that gave Claire the strength to answer back.

"And, of course, you have paternity test results available to back that up, have you? Because a lot can happen in one year, you realize," Claire said calmly, and returned Gen's scheming stare, steadily. The other woman's eye-contact faltered, and Gen glanced down at her lap.

"No, no paternity test yet. I am hoping that Richard will come back to me voluntarily, without us having to resort to such crude methods."

"Hold on. So, you're telling me that you want Richard to give up the life he's created for himself over the past year, pretend it never happened and his mom isn't ill, and return with you to Montreal on the suggestion that your baby 'might' be his? A baby that he doesn't even know exists?" Claire couldn't keep her voice from rising as she said this. She noticed the Uber driver looking back at them using his rearview mirror.

"Yes, and no, but there is no need for you to be sarcastic and unpleasant." Geneviève looked out of the window. "Here we are at the hotel, please wait until we are inside."

Claire couldn't wait to jump out of the Uber. The vehicle's heater fan was blasting on full, and the interior suddenly felt claustrophobic and oppressive. She walked to the driver's side and paid him. He gave her a compassionate nod after she had given him a tip and rated him five stars. He watched the two ladies walk into the hotel lobby before driving off. The one was tall, slim, and had long, wild, red hair that reached down to her waist. The other lady had an unshakeable air of self-possession about her, which was not diminished by her tiny stature at all. The driver silently wished the tall redhead good luck.

Geneviève walked to the reception desk with her head held high. She had the kind of face that always looked as though she wore a slight smile.

Body language experts would have a field day with her, trying to work out if she is genuinely happy causing me this much discomfort or whether she's just ignorant of other people's feelings.

Claire stayed close to Geneviève. She wanted to check the number of her hotel room. It might be necessary to leave telephonic messages for her later on.

"I'm here to check in, if you please," Gen said brightly to the reception clerk, "I dropped my suitcases off here earlier but didn't have time to check in."

The clerk nodded, "Yes, ma'am. We have your suitcases waiting and your room card ready for you. Please go straight up to the fourth floor, room four-o-seven. The concierge will bring your luggage to your room shortly."

"No, thank you. I would like to have a coffee first," Geneviève said regally, as the clerk handed her credit card and passport back to her. She jerked her head at Claire, indicating she should follow her to the coffee shop.

After they had settled themselves down at an elegant maroon highbacked banquette booth, Claire spoke out, "I couldn't help but notice that you returned to Richard's parents' house before even checking in."

"Yes," Gen replied brightly, "I was waiting in a taxicab across the road when you both arrived. You didn't see me because I ducked down when you drove past."

"Why would you want to do that?" Claire was beginning to find this little woman's actions as unfathomable as her motives.

"It suited my purposes to do so," Geneviève said, and took a nibble of biscotti.

"Can I see pictures of the baby?" Claire wondered how old the baby was and what it looked like.

Gen fiddled with her phone for a minute and then handed it over to Claire. She saw an unsmiling infant of about four or five months old on the screen. She handed the phone back to Gen, at a loss for words.

"Er, um, it's got dark hair," she eventually said. Richard had white-blond hair that reminded most people of Nordic Viking warriors.

"Yes, he is just like his mother," Gen replied, completely unfazed by Claire's comment.

Claire hadn't ordered anything, and felt it was time for her to leave. She didn't think she could take much more of this cruel game of cat and mouse. Fighting back the impulse to flee, Claire stiffened her resolve and made her farewell speech, "Geneviève, Richard told me a bit about his relationship with you. He was young, alone, and far from home when he met you. He has freely admitted to me that you have a wonderful family and lovely home. You were all nice enough to welcome him in and treat him with kindness. Your father helped Richard get his first job, your lives probably looked as though they were set to be intertwined forever. Right?"

Geneviève sat across from Claire with a stony expression. She made no response to Claire's question.

Bravely, Claire soldiered on.

"The thing is, Gen, people evolve all the time. I'm sure that you aren't the same girl who began dating Richard when he was still in law school. What is it that you do now?"

Geneviève gave a chuffing sound through her lips, "Idiot. I do mothering, now. I have a baby, Richard's baby, to look after."

Claire bit back an acidic retort, yet, patronizing Gen, acknowledged, "Of course you do. Good for you. However, Richard has changed. He wants to help his father look after his mother. No baby is going to change that. And he wants to be with me. We're taking our relationship one day at a time, but so far, it's worked out well for us."

"You are not connected to Richard enough to be permanent," Geneviève retorted unequivocally, "I was his girlfriend for eight years, his fiancée, and now I'm the mother of his child. You are a ship passing us in the night, and it will be better for everyone if you just keep on sailing by."

Angry red blotches appeared on Claire's cheekbones. Geneviève gave her an enigmatic smile, obviously hoping she had scored a hit.

Claire swallowed, and continued, enunciating calmly and rationally, as though trying to make a toddler see reason, "Gen, please don't be mean. At the very most, we should be discussing how you can move here with the baby, to Sydney. Richard can help you find accommodation close to his work or his parents' house. He can pay child support if the baby proves to be his. There are many options open to you, to us. Ones that don't involve him marrying you."

Gen's implacable smile never left her face. "Maybe so, maybe I will do that. Just think Miss Claire Havisham, I will be here with Richard every day. I have his beautiful son for him to call his own. I can look after his mother, give Mr. Benson a break from all this nursing. They will love me for it, you do realize? While you are sulking and skulking over in Pleasant Bay in that cottage with the stupid name. How do you rate your chances of outlasting me, hey?"

"I rate my chances as pretty high, Gen. I'll be sure to get my relationship with Richard right the first time around. I won't need to try and get a second chance, as you are attempting."

"It's you who are mistaken, dear," Gen remarked off-handedly, "I don't need a second chance with Richard because I'm still on my first chance with him. You're just a glitch."

Claire got up, pulled on her overcoat, and walked out of the coffee shop without looking back.

She hailed a taxicab at the rank outside and gave the driver

Richard's parents' address. During the drive, the red flush left Claire's cheeks, and she pressed her forehead against the side window to keep cool and avoid the heat that blasted from the fans. She managed to order her chaotic thoughts as the cab made its way along George Street and on toward the Bensons' home.

The first thing she saw when the car pulled up at the curb was Richard's anxious face framed in the bay window next to his mother's. She paid the driver and began walking wearily up the pathway to the front door.

I should be hungry. It's nearly time for dinner. But even though I feel empty, I'm not hungry. How strange.

Bo opened the door for Claire before she knocked. He helped her take off her coat and waited for her to kick off her boots. She followed him into the lounge. Instinctively, Claire waited to see if Richard's mother would recognize her.

"Hello, Claire," Mrs. Benson said with a welcoming smile.

Claire ran into Richard's mother's arms and hugged her affectionately. She couldn't help tears from welling up, but now was no time for that. She reached into her coat pocket, took out her phone, and pressed the "Play" icon.

The sound of Gen's voice filled the cozy sitting room.

"Thank you for accompanying me. Can you keep a secret? I need to have Richard back as my husband because we have a baby together."

Chapter Six: This Game Must Play Out

A hush fell over the room as everyone listened to Claire's recording of her conversation with Gen. Only when the grating of static could be heard did Claire close her recording app.

"She sounds like a right piece of work," Brigitte Benson said with conviction.

"I agree," said her husband, "but I think we have a handle on her now and can discuss more about this over supper. I have a nice soup and homemade bread going. Shall we eat in here?"

"Yes, please, Dad," Richard chipped in, "do you need any help in the kitchen?"

Claire was a bit surprised at how calmly everyone in the Benson household was taking this.

"Richard! She says you are the father of her son! Doesn't that disturb you at all?"

Richard was watching his dad, who indicated he didn't need help in the kitchen with a shake of his head, then he turned back to look at Claire, "Darling, I'm a lawyer. When I wasn't a lawyer, I was studying to be one. Believe me when I say that there was no way Gen would have been able to get pregnant when we were together. Studying paternity suits and a father's financial and legal responsibilities for three years—well, suffice to say that it's enough to make any young man think twice and practice caution."

"Hear, hear!" chimed in Bo from the kitchen.

"I've read that there's a two percent chance of failure." Claire could remember her own dilemmas as a student and also knew the statistics like the back of her hand. "Isn't that enough to make you worry?'

Richard sighed and got up out of his comfortable armchair to come and sit cross-legged in front of where Claire was sitting, "Claire Bear, sure there's a one in a trillion chance that I got a faulty batch—even though every single one is tested before being accepted and sold—but can't you see, Gen's whole reason for waiting until she had you alone in the taxicab before telling you this was in the hope of scaring *you* off and not to bring me closer."

Bo Benson returned to the sitting room with a large soup tureen in his hands. "Go and get the bread and butter, will you please, Son?"

Richard got up, patted Claire knees, gave them a quick squeeze, and then went out to the kitchen. When he came back with the bread on a board and butter crock, he placed them on the coffee table around which they were gathered and carried on talking while they ate.

"Is that why you allowed me to go off to the hotel with her? To see if she would try one of her scare tactics on me?" Claire sounded skeptical. She could think of far easier ways to flush out Gen's ruthless methods to get Richard back then putting them alone in a room together. "Why didn't you just ask her straight out 'what's your game?' and force her to reveal her hand or get out of our lives forever."

"I actually don't want to do that until I have first double-checked my dates and alibis regarding her accusation. If you all don't mind, I'm going to give Miss Allaire a phone call after supper and ask her for the baby's date of birth. If she tries to dodge around providing me with that, we'll know immediately that she's full of sh-nonsense."

Richard stumbled over his last words and gave his mother a look to see if she'd noticed his slip. Brigitte was contentedly sipping her soup and watching a ballroom dance competition on the television that was playing softly in the background.

Richard gave a silent whistle of relief and pretended to wipe sweat off his brow, "Mom's super-strict when it comes to swearing," he whispered as an aside to Claire, "she used to ask me to wash my mouth out with vinegar when I was a teenager."

Claire bubbled over with suppressed mirth at the thought of a tall, muscular thirty-year-old Richard being forced to gargle with vinegar by the petite Brigitte. They spent the rest of the meal whispering about the kind of disciplinary methods their parents had used on them as children and laughing merrily about the various ingenious ways their mothers had enforced the rules of the house. Geneviève's unwelcome visit was forgotten, until after dinner.

Richard and Claire went through to his bedroom and shut the door. They got ready for bed quickly, each taking their turn in the guest bathroom and then running back quickly to the room holding a bath bag. Claire changed into comfortable sweats and Richard pulled off his outerwear to reveal a white long-sleeved T-shirt and long johns. They jumped under the duck down duvet and Richard leaned over to adjust the electric blanket thermostat.

Claire watched as Richard pressed Gen's number.

He held up his finger to Claire when Gen answered, to alert her that he'd activated speaker phone.

"Allô, Richard. Are you calling to wish me bonne nuit?" Gen's voice sounded sultry and teasing.

"Yes, of course I wish you a very good night, Gen, and hopefully we can be wishing you a bon voyage and adieu soon too, when you go back home." Claire could see from the expression on Richard's face that he was through with playing games. "But that's not the reason for this call, as of course I'm sure you know. I want the baby's date of birth, please. And can a copy of the birth certificate be sent to me as soon as possible while you're at it?"

After a brief pause, Gen replied, "Ahh, our baby's date of birth was on the nineteenth of September, last year."

"Great," Richard sounded officious and business-like, "and in which hospital was he born? Better yet, just send the hospital records over to me and I'll check them myself. I'll also be sending over a professional DNA consultant to Montreal to take a swab. Will you be there, or can someone stand in for you in a legal capacity? It'll be filmed and recorded on both sides, so that there can be no accusation of fraud or contamination. Who shall I contact to organize that, please?"

It was a subtly aggressive barrage of enquiry. At that moment, Claire was able to see what a formidable opponent Richard might be in a court of law.

After a considerable pause, Gen spoke, "You go too fast, Richard, can't we just enjoy this moment first? Why do you have to be so abrupt when I swear to you that this baby is yours. Is that not enough for us, after all that we have been together? How—"

"I'm going to stop you right there, Gen," Richard interrupted, "you don't get to ask me questions, do you understand? Even if those questions are being phrased in a reminiscent fashion, it only serves to show me that you are being economical with the truth and with the facts."

"That little baby is yours, and if you want to deny it, then I will sue you for breach of promise to me, and seduction, and—and misrepresentation! You don't get to tell me what to do!" All the sweetness and lightness had disappeared from Gen's voice. It croaked harshly and noisily over the small phone speaker.

"In which hospital was the baby born?" Richard was like a battering ram; he would not be put off in his search for the truth. "If you are not more forthcoming with information, I'm going to end this conversation now."

"Okay, okay, I gave birth to little Alexandre at Sainte-Justine's." Gen obviously knew when she had reached the limits of Richard's patience. "But I did not put you down as his father, because I wanted to speak with you first, y'know, get back together."

"A very optimistic way of looking at things, Gen. I will expect your babysitter, or whoever is looking after Alexandre while you are here, to await a visit from my representative. Can I know what phone number they can call to make an appointment ahead of time?'

"Uh, I'll send it to you by text Richard." For the first time since meeting Gen, Claire was able to hear hesitance in her voice, "Look out for my text, chéri." Gen disconnected the call.

Claire blew a small gust of air out of her lungs and collapsed down onto Richard's bed. "I feel as though we're up against one of those awful false accusations that are made and can tarnish a person's reputation before the true facts are known—you know the ones I'm talking about?"

Richard lay down beside Claire on the bed and put his arm underneath her neck, "Yes, I understand the feeling you have. Fortunately, Gen is savvy enough not to go public in any capacity with her lies, because then I'll be the one to gain the upper hand. I would be able to sue her from here to next Sunday if she made these unsubstantiated claims in a public forum."

Claire loved listening to the sound of Richard's voice as she lay against his chest. She could hear the deep rumble of what he was saying vibrating, and it lulled her jumbled thoughts.

How lucky I am to be with such a levelheaded guy. Nothing seems to upset him or catch him off balance. He looks at every problem in a logical way.

Richard gave Claire a gentle prod. "You still awake, sleepy-head?"

Claire gave a small chuckle and mumbled a soft 'yes.'

"I want to thank you so much for standing by me and believing in me through all of this," Richard said, his voice growing gruff with emotion, "you have shown me what a strong, intelligent woman you are, Claire, and it makes me love you even more, if that were possible. Knowing you are standing by me, as we let Gen's game play out, makes me so happy."

Claire gave a tiny murmur of protest and turned to press her body against Richard's. It was their favorite sleeping position. He had his arm under her neck and Claire had her body pressed sideways against his, her arm draped over his chest. Sometimes, she would wrap her leg over his thighs for extra warmth and comfort.

It's the perfect sleeping position for a cold winter's night. I feel safe and loved when I'm in Richard's arms.

Claire's thoughts were happy ones as she drifted off to sleep.

Chapter Seven: Secrets Revealed

The next morning, Richard leaned over to the end table next to the bed and checked his text messages the minute he woke. Notification alerts pinged and beeped a few seconds after he'd deactivated the Do Not Disturb icon. While Richard flicked through his communications, Claire took the opportunity to sneak away to the bathroom for a quick shower. She hated Richard seeing her in the morning without her mascara on.

When she returned to the bedroom, Richard was speaking to someone on the phone.

"Well, call it before booking a flight, but give them the wrong date and time in case they try to duck and dive you after your arrival. Record everything. Thanks, cheers."

Richard looked at Claire as she breezed back into the room, "You appear to be completely recovered from the terrible day we had yesterday," he commented happily.

Claire pulled back the drapes to check if any snow had fallen during the night, before answering, "I feel marvelous. I slept like a log and now I'm ready to face anything the world wants to throw at me."

"It's good to hear you say that, darling. That was the guy I use to collect evidence boxes for me. He's part of a delivery chain making sure samples and clues aren't contaminated. He says he can fly over and do the swab test today. I have to go into the office but should be able to clear my desk by lunchtime, hopefully. Are you going to be okay staying here with Mom and Dad?'

Claire was tempted to snuggle back under the duvet and ask Richard to spend the day with her, cozy and warm in bed. But she nodded her head, saying, "Uh-huh, sure thing babe," while putting on her sexy mohair boat-necked pullover that draped provocatively over one shoulder and pushing her legs into a skin-tight pair of leggings.

Sometimes a girl just has to put in a bit of effort to make herself feel ready to face the day.

Claire couldn't help smiling to herself as Richard observed her outfit with more than a look of admiration. She gave him a cheeky wink and went out to the breakfast nook.

Bo Benson was already up and preparing a bowl of cereal for himself and Brigitte. He motioned to Claire to make herself at home in the kitchen, and then walked through to the lounge with the two bowls in his hands. Claire crossed her fingers under her long sleeves and prayed that Mrs. Benson was having a good day. After pouring herself a large mug of hot coffee, Claire went to join Richard's parents in the sitting room.

The Bensons were seated side by side in the bay window nook. Brigitte had a small white rectangle of cardboard in her hand, and both her and Bo were engrossed in the message written on the card. Bo looked up as she walked in and Claire was aware of how like his father Richard looked.

"'You and me are meant to be together,'—who wrote you this sappy piece of nonsense, Claire?"

Claire dragged a small ottoman closer to the bay window and

sat down on it, nursing her mug of coffee between her hands. "I don't know. It's a bit of a mystery. Messages like that started arriving after I moved to Songbird Cottage. Richard said it might be ominous, but then how come no one has come forward to claim them?"

"There's a bear on the card. Who else knows that your mother and Richard like to call you 'Bear'?" Bo was frowning as he concentrated on the card, turning it from front to back as though it might hold a clue.

"Perhaps the florist just thought it looked cute," Claire mumbled, her mug of coffee forgotten on the carpet below her.

Richard came into the room to hug his mother goodbye and give Claire a loving kiss. "Be good. I'll see you at lunch." He waved farewell, giving Claire that gorgeous smile she adored so much as he went out the door.

Bo watched his son leave, and then stretched out his hand to Claire, "We are going to be busy this morning, Claire. We are going to document every single message and email that you have sent since leaving Bangor to come and live at Cape Breton. And we aren't going to stop until we find out who this person is. Give me your phone, because that's a good place to start."

The Bensons and Claire moved to the formal dining room to organize things for their search. The morning passed quickly as Claire read aloud the messages she'd sent and received, the information the messages contained, and the dates.

Halfway through the morning, the sound of a car pulling up

outside was heard. Bo Benson scrunched up his eyes as though he was in physical pain, "If that's Geneviève Allaire, I'll hit the roof!"

Brigitte Benson had been seated quietly beside him all morning, but at the sound of her husband swearing, she was galvanized into action. She smacked the side of his upper arm, exclaiming, "No swearing in my house, Bo!"

The doorbell rang, and Bo was grateful to get up and answer the door while his wife apologized to Claire for his outburst. He returned carrying a blooming orchid wrapped in the finest pink tissue wrapping. Claire reached out to take the white card he held out to her. She opened the envelope, and read out the message aloud, "'You and me should spend Valentine's Day together. Shall we meet up on the fourteenth?' That's all it says." Claire was glad she was sitting down, as all the strength seemed to have drained out of her legs.

Bo was jubilant, "We've got them now! And we don't have to go all the way back through all your messages to find out who it is. Who did you tell that you are leaving Pleasant Bay and coming here, Claire?"

Claire scrolled down to the messages and emails she had been sending back and forth since leaving Songbird Cottage the previous morning. She read out the names, and Bo jotted them down.

"Mom, of course. Izzy, in Manhattan. I texted Sam to ask him when the next batch of honey would be ready for shipping. Um, um…" Claire felt the excitement grow as she got closer to the truth, "Della, one of the freelancers who used to rent a treatment room from me in Bangor—hang on, I didn't tell her I was coming here…"

Claire froze and then read out a message, "'Hi Edie. This is just to let you know that I'm leaving to stay in Sydney for a few days.

I'll forward a landline number to you; someone called Mr. Benson will answer if you call there. Thanks, C.'"

"Who's Edie?" Bo asked.

"Edie Grady. She is the manager at my salon in Bangor. She was slightly injured when my ex-boyfriend's mother crashed her car through the salon's sidewalk window. There are still all kinds of legal issues to be sorted out, so I left her in charge, still on salary, so that I could come and live here. I tell her pretty much everything that I do. I didn't tell her about becoming Richard's girlfriend though, because I try to keep my personal life out of business relationships."

A heavy silence fell over the formal dining room. Brigitte was staring blankly at the potted orchid on the table. Bo had his head down, and he appeared to be deep in thought. Finally, he raised his head, and asked Claire, "Do you still have that lady's reference letters and résumé? I'm assuming you didn't hire her without them?"

Claire rose and went to Richard's room to retrieve her laptop. She came back into the room, pulled the laptop out of its casing, and opened it up on the table. Bo waited patiently for Claire to find the correct documents file.

"Here it is. I called that number" She leaned over the table and indicated to Bo which one. "The man had only good things to say about her. She moved all the way from New York to Bangor to work for me, and it was only part-time in the beginning."

Bo frowned as he read the documents, "And that didn't sound any warning bells with you? The fact that this woman was willing to leave New York for only a part-time job? Did she mention having family there? Someone to support her while she worked part-time?"

"Nooooo…" Claire replied doubtfully, "but her boss wrote on his letter of recommendation that he was sad to lose her. When I called that number, it was his private line, I think."

"Really?" Bo sounded as sarcastic, even as an elderly man, "Don't you know that's the oldest trick in the book, giving a cell phone number instead of one belonging to a bricks and mortar establishment."

Claire dropped her head in shame.

This was my first business, and I thought I knew how to run things. Now, boy, do I feel stupid.

"Don't blame yourself, Claire," Bo Benson reassured her, "Plenty of first-time business owners have done far worse for themselves. Let's call this number, shall we?"

Bo got up from the table and went to get the landline phone from the hutch behind him. He came back to the table, sat back down, and dialed the number while checking every few digits to see he had it right. Just like his son the night before, he pushed speaker when a voice answered, "Jake Cartmel speaking."

"Hello, good morning, Mr. Cartmel. I'm calling from the insurance company regarding all the claims made by Ms. Edie Grady for her injuries and losses after the salon in Bangor was destroyed." He waited to hear Mr. Cartmel's response before continuing. The man on the other end of the line just grunted in the affirmative. "Thank you, Mr. Cartmel for giving me some of your valuable time. I just want to make sure that Ms. Grady has never made any similar claims against you or your salon? Your number is here as her previous employer."

"What? Oh yeah, well don't bother me with any of this again. If you need info about Edie just call Simpson, Everett, and Delgado, and ask for Charles du Pont. He can handle any enquiries, okay? Hey, why are you calling from an international number?"

"Our head office is offshore, Mr. Cartmel. Thank you for your time."

Bo hung up the phone. He got up from the table and went to the kitchen to get Claire a glass of water. She had gone as pale as a ghost when she'd heard the man give the details over the phone. When he came back and handed her the glass, he asked if she would like to go and lie down, "Or are you going to be the brave girl I know you to be and tell me what it is you just realized?"

Claire wanted to be brave, she really did. But only half truths would do until she'd been able to marshal her thoughts into less of a chaotic mess.

"Bo, I'm sorry to act like such a drama queen. Matter of fact, I know the firm of Simpson, Everett, and Delgado very well. My stepbrother is a junior partner there. He hasn't worked there long enough to be a named partner, like Richard, but he is definitely still working there."

Bo sat down heavily. His wife turned from the window and looked over at him with a worried expression on her face. Claire cleared her throat loudly so that Mr. Benson would know his wife had picked up on the unsettled environment in the room. He sat up, thanked Claire with a quick nod and took Brigitte out of the room. Claire heard him close their bedroom door. She was left alone with her thoughts until the sound of Richard's key was heard in the door.

I know Bo would have texted Richard. Now I must be prepared to tell my story. For how long have I kept this a secret? But if Richard and I have a chance of moving forward, I have to be honest with him.

Richard came into the dining room. His face showed concern and worry, but no other emotion. "Claire Bear, my Dad told me who might have been sending you the gifts and flowers and also how he was getting the information about your movements. Do you want to talk about it?"

Claire took a deep breath, "Yes, love, I do want to tell you about it—everything. I've kept this a secret for far too long. The only thing I ask is that you don't tell my Mom a word about what's said in here. It stays within these four walls. Understand?"

Richard said, "If that's the case, why don't we go into my bedroom? Then Dad can make lunch, and we won't be overheard."

Claire followed Richard into the bedroom, and he shut the door behind him. "Shoot," he said and sat down on the bed next to Claire. She preferred that, as she was able to tell her story without having to look up and see him.

Claire had suppressed her memories for a long time. It had been around the same time her mother had stopped bringing them to Songbird Cottage for summer holidays. Her father had married his mistress, then girlfriend, Linette, and they were making the move to Halifax, Nova Scotia from Manhattan together. It was a time of turmoil. Linette was suddenly more than just her father's girlfriend on the side. She had complete authority around the house and over John's two daughters. Claire and Izzy had been living a straddled existence between their mother's apartment in Tribeca and their father, John's, luxury shorefront mansion at Northwest Arm.

Living together had worked perfectly at first. The house in Halifax was large enough for the girls to avoid Linette whenever she was in a bad mood. And Linette cooked nice food, which was always a welcome thing for two young girls. Claire had been fourteen and Izzy nearly ten years old. They had hung out in their rooms or gone out to the many attractions and places of interest in and around Halifax.

Then Linette's two sons had arrived to live with her.

It had been bearable in the beginning. The house still felt spacious enough for four teenagers. Linette's youngest son was the same age as Claire but had been so socially gauche that he kept to his room and played video games all day. Then Charles du Pont had arrived, Linette's eldest son. He was studying for his LSATs and had come to Nova Scotia to see his mother's new house. Initially, Claire had thought it exciting to have an older boy living in the same house as she did. She found it very glamorous that Chucky du Pont wanted to spend time with her, little unsophisticated Claire Havisham. It seemed completely natural to spend every day with him, getting him to rent age-restricted movies for her from the rental store and giggling together on the couch while they watched them.

"Then Dad and Linette went away for a holiday trip, and left Chuck in charge. And that was when he started to mess around with me – sexually. I didn't feel comfortable with it and asked him to stop, but it fell on deaf ears. He had a way of making it feel half like a game, and half like I would get into trouble if I didn't do it. I can't explain it better than that."

Claire realized she was whispering and raised her voice so that Richard would know she was not ashamed to tell these things to the man she loved.

"When Dad came back from his vacation, I went to his clinic in town and told him I wanted to go back to Mom's. He didn't ask any questions. Why should he? He thought I was homesick. Chuck tried visiting and calling a few times, but Mom hates him and told him to stop bothering me. She thought he was a creep. I never told Mom either. She felt guilty enough for divorcing Dad when she found out about Linette. I didn't want to lay even more troubles on her."

"I think you are the bravest woman, and the most considerate one, I have ever met, Claire," Richard whispered, reverently.

She turned toward him and buried her face in his chest. Richard stroked her hair.

"Things like this happen to children all the time, Claire," he said, "It was highly irresponsible of your father to surmise that you girls would be treated like sisters by a couple of adolescent youths with whom you hadn't grown up."

"Dad can be a bit selfish, at times, Richard, but I think he's finally started to put other people first in his old age. Look what he did for my mom after her second husband stole all her money.'

Richard scoffed, "A bit too late for you to be saved by his overdue altruism, don't you agree?"

"I've made my peace with it a long time ago. I asked Dad to set me up with a shrink because I was troubled over the divorce, and so I was able to work through things with the help of lovely Dr. Metcalf. She said I would tell someone when I was good and ready. And so…"

Richard swept Claire into his arms and held her tightly. She felt her heart give a leap of happiness when he looked deeply into her eyes with his own crystal-clear turquoise ones. The connection between them was so intense and strong that Claire was not sure if it was her own pulse she felt beating, or Richard's. All of her worries and bad memories were pushed out of her mind when he fastened his lips to hers and kissed her with a passion that took her breath away—time lost all meaning as Claire gave herself over to the ecstatic feeling of loving and being loved. Winter would always be warm within Richard's arms.

"Oh, Richard," Claire gasped as she broke away, "my head's spinning! What about going to help your dad prepare lunch. Have you eaten?"

"Forget about lunch, Claire Havisham. I have decided that you are more important to me than food, or work, or oxygen, for that matter! Will you do me the incredible honor of becoming my wife? I want to make sure I can love and protect you forever."

Claire had never heard those words of such promise before in her life. She sat quietly for a moment and allowed the wondrous feeling of being unconditionally loved to wash over her like a cleansing balm.

I never want to spend my life with anyone else by my side except Richard.

Claire became aware that Richard was looking at her with a slightly apprehensive look on his face. She burst into laughter and flung herself into his arms.

"Yes, my darling, yes! Of course, I want to be your wife!"

Find out how the story ends in Seasons at *Songbird Cottage* (Pleasant Bay Book 5).

Seasons at
Songbird
Cottage
BOOK FIVE
A PLEASANT BAY
NOVEL
SYLVIA PRICE

With her life in shambles, and with nowhere else to stay, Emma returns to Songbird Cottage. Despite leaving without an explanation eighteen years ago, Sam is quick to Emma's aid when she arrives on Cape Breton.

As the beauty and peacefulness of Pleasant Bay begin to heal Emma, she gets some shocking news, and she discovers that she's unwelcomed at Songbird Cottage. Will she be able to piece her life back together and get another chance at happiness?

Return To Songbird Cottage (Pleasant Bay Book 2)

When Emma Copeland loses everything, she returns to her former vacation home, Songbird Cottage, in Pleasant Bay, Cape Breton Island as a last resort. While Emma tries to piece her life back together, she reconnects with Sam MacAuley, an old neighbor and friend.

As Emma's relationship with Sam begins to deepen, her first husband, Dr. John Havisham, tells her that he wants to return to Songbird Cottage as well, and he brings their youngest daughter, Isabelle, with him. On top of that, someone clearly doesn't want Emma in Pleasant Bay. Will Sam and Emma's budding relationship withstand these complications?

Secrets Of Songbird Cottage (Pleasant Bay Book 4)

Claire Havisham is enjoying her first winter at Songbird Cottage. As her relationship with her boyfriend, Richard Benson, is warming up, they discover that they've both been keeping secrets from each other.

Claire has been receiving gifts and packages from a secret admirer, but she doesn't want anyone to know. Richard, who had left Montreal to move back home to Cape Breton Island to help care for his ailing mother, drops a bombshell on Claire when he announces that his fiancée, Geneviève Allaire, has arrived in town. Can Claire and Richard's relationship survive these secrets?

Seasons At Songbird Cottage (Pleasant Bay Book 5)

Emma Copeland's family and friends are gathering at Songbird Cottage for a special celebration in honor of her eldest daughter, Claire. Everyone, except for Emma's youngest daughter Isabelle, is excited to see each other again. Izzy was an aspiring musician, but since her band broke up, her life has been in a downward spiral. Her self-destructive behavior worries Emma and Claire, but they are at a loss as to what to do when Izzy runs back to New York.

With no one in her family able to help her, Emma's husband, Sam, sends his youngest son Luke, a childhood friend of Izzy's, to bring her back to Songbird Cottage. The cottage had been a place of healing for both Emma and Claire. Will Izzy accept Luke's help and let Songbird Cottage work its magic?

Jonah's Redemption: Book 1 (An Amish Romance)

FREE ON AMAZON!

Jonah has lost his community, and he's struggling to get by in the English world. He yearns for his Amish roots, but his past mistakes keep him from returning home.

Mary Lou is recovering from a medical scare. Her journey has impressed upon her how precious life is, so she decides to go on rumspringa to see the world.

While in the city, Mary Lou meets Jonah. Unable to understand his foul attitude, especially towards her, she makes every effort to share her faith with him. As she helps him heal from his past, an attraction develops.

Will Jonah's heart soften towards Mary Lou? What will God do with these two broken people?

Jonah's Redemption: Boxed Set (An Amish Romance)

If you loved Jonah's Redemption: Book 1 (available for free on Amazon), grab the rest of the series in this special boxed set featuring Books 2-5, plus a bonus epilogue and companion story.

Mary Lou's fiancé leaves her as soon as tragedy strikes. Unwilling to resent him, she chooses, instead, to find him. Her misfortunes pile up in her quest to return Jonah to the Amish faith, but she is undeterred, for God has given her a mission.

Will Mary Lou's faith be enough to help them get through the countless obstacles that are thrown their way? Do Jonah and Mary Lou have a chance at happiness?

Join Jonah and Mary Lou as they wrestle with love, a life worth living, and their unique faith in Christ. Enjoy the conclusion of Jonah's Redemption in this exclusive boxed set, with a bonus epilogue and companion story!

The Christmas Arrival: An Amish Holiday Romance

Rachel Lapp is a young Amish woman who is the daughter of the community's bishop. She is in the midst of planning the annual Christmas Nativity play when newcomer Noah Miller arrives in town to spend Christmas with his cousins. Encouraged by her father to welcome the new arrival, Rachel asks Noah to be a part of the Nativity.

Despite Rachel's engagement to Samuel King, a local farmer, she finds herself irrevocably drawn to Noah and his carefree spirit. Reserved and slightly shy, Noah is hesitant to get involved in the play, but an unlikely friendship begins to develop between Rachel and Noah, bringing with it unexpected problems, including a seemingly harmless prank with life-threatening consequences that require a Christmas miracle.

Will Rachel honor her commitment to Samuel, or will Noah win her affections?

Join these characters on what is sure to be a heartwarming holiday adventure! Instead of waiting for each part to be released, enjoy the entire Christmas Arrival series in this exclusive collection!

About the Author

Now an Amazon bestselling author, Sylvia Price is an author of Amish and contemporary romance and women's fiction. She especially loves writing uplifting stories about second chances!

Although raised in the cosmopolitan city of Montréal, Sylvia spent her adolescent and young adult years in Nova Scotia, and the beautiful countryside landscapes and ocean views serve as the backdrop to her contemporary novels.

After meeting and falling in love with an American while living abroad, Sylvia now resides in the US. She spends her days writing, hoping to inspire the next generation to read more stories. When she's not writing, Sylvia stays busy making sure her three young children are alive and well-fed.

Subscribe to Sylvia's newsletter at newsletter.sylviaprice.com to stay in the loop about new releases, freebies, promos, and more. As a thank-you, you will receive a FREE exclusive short story that isn't available for purchase.

Learn more about Sylvia at amazon.com/author/sylviaprice and goodreads.com/author/show/1134593.Sylvia_Price.

Follow Sylvia on Facebook at facebook.com/sylviapriceauthor for updates.

Join Sylvia's Advanced Reader Copies (ARC) team at arcteam.sylviaprice.com to get her books for free before they are released in exchange for honest reviews.